X-Treme Sports

BMX Biking

K.E. Vieregger

ABDO Publishing Company

visit us at
www.abdopub.com

Published by ABDO Publishing Company, 4940 Viking Drive, Edina, Minnesota 55435.
Copyright © 2003 by Abdo Consulting Group, Inc. International copyrights reserved in all
countries. No part of this book may be reproduced in any form without written permission from
the publisher.

Printed in the United States.

Cover Photo: Corbis
Interior Photos: Corbis pp. 4, 5, 6, 7, 9, 10, 11, 13, 14, 15, 17, 19, 20, 21, 24, 26-27, 28, 29, 31

Editors: Kate A. Conley, Stephanie Hedlund, Jennifer R. Krueger
Art Direction: Neil Klinepier

Library of Congress Cataloging-in-Publication Data

Vieregger, K. E., 1978-
  BMX biking / K. E. Vieregger.
      p. cm. -- (X-treme sports)
  Includes index.
  Summary: Presents the history, needed equipment, and various techniques of bicycle
moto-cross racing.
  ISBN 1-57765-926-0
    1. Bicycle motocross--Juvenile literature. [1. Bicycle motocross.] I. Title. II Title: Bicycle
motocross biking. III. Series.

  GV1049.3 .V83 2003
  796.6'2--dc21

                                                                2002026095

Contents

BMX Biking

Would you like to fly through the air off a quarter-pipe ramp? Or would you rather corner a berm at full speed? BMX bikers are doing this and more, and they are having a blast! In competitions and recreational events, BMX bikers are gaining attention.

The letters BMX stand for bicycle motocross. Bicycle motocross is a style of racing. But BMX bikers do more than race. Many bikers take part in freestyle competitions. And many young riders use their BMX bikes every day, just to get from place to place.

BMX biking began in the 1960s. At first, boys were most often seen at competitions. But today, boys, girls, men, and women enjoy the excitement of BMX. They enjoy watching, competing, or just cruising on a BMX bike.

BMX is a great sport because almost anyone can learn to ride a bicycle. But even if you are just watching a competition, BMX biking is thrilling.

BMX Begins

The first bicycle was made in 1839. A blacksmith in Scotland built this bicycle, but it never became popular. Then in 1861, two Frenchmen built a new **version** of the bicycle. It grew in popularity and appeared in the United States in 1866.

Bicycling used to be an activity for adults only. That's because early bicycles were heavy and difficult to ride. But throughout the 1890s, people improved the bicycle. This allowed children to enjoy riding them, too!

By the 1960s, U.S. children loved to bicycle. Some of them dreamed of one day riding a motorcycle. These children imitated motorcycle **stunts** on their bicycles. They tried to pop wheelies and fly

This early version of the bicycle was called the boneshaker.

around corners. But the bikes broke easily because they were not made to withstand this rough treatment. Despite this, children continued to race and perform on their bikes.

In 1970, the first neighborhood BMX race was held in California. Thirteen-year-old Scot Breithaupt organized the event. There were 35 racers the first weekend. The next weekend, 150 racers joined the fun. Soon, racetracks were forming all over the United States. The first official race was held in California, in 1971.

A Schwinn bicycle from the early 1950s

That same year, the bicycle manufacturer Schwinn created a bike that was sturdy and could handle extra bouncing and harsh treatment. This bike was called the Stingray. It was featured in the movie called *On Any Sunday*.

Children all over the United States watched *On Any Sunday*. The movie was mainly about motorcycles. But there was a scene where children rode around on their specially made bicycles. They were performing tricks just like the motorcycle riders!

Many children wanted one of those tough bikes so they could race and do **stunts**, too. Others just wanted a sturdy bike that they could ride anywhere. A new **craze** began in the United States. It became known as BMX.

Throughout the 1970s, many BMX organizations developed. They all held their own races. As a result, racing rules differed depending on where and when the race was held.

Then in 1974, the National Bicycle League (NBL) formed, and BMX became an official sport. A set of rules and a standard track were established. Standards for bikes and safety equipment were set, too.

Soon, riders traveled all over the United States to compete in races. Sometimes the riders received money for winning competitions. Other times, the riders won **trophies**.

New bikes were also created and **marketed** at this time. Bicycle manufacturers tried to make the bikes look like motorcycles. The bikes looked cool, but they were too big and heavy for racing.

Motocross racers line up to begin a race in 1975.

In order to be fast, bicycles need to be light. So some bikers stripped down their bikes to make them lighter. To do this, they removed parts that were just decorations. They also removed parts that were heavy or not necessary, such as kickstands and mudguards. Eventually, companies came out with sturdy, lightweight racing bikes.

Soon, BMX bikers formed one organization to regulate racing rules around the world. The first International BMX Federation (IBMXF) meeting was held in October 1981. It celebrated the tenth year of BMX. IBMXF held international races and a world championship. Since then, BMX racing has continued to grow in popularity. The X Games and Gravity Games have helped expose the sport worldwide. And organizations, such as the NBL, continue to hold races in the United States.

BMX racetracks often have puddles, hills, and other obstacles.

Bike Basics

The most important piece of equipment for a BMX biker is the bike. Most BMX bikes have the same shape as a motorcycle. Several main parts make up a BMX bike. They are the frame, handlebars, stem, wheels, drivetrain, seat, and brakes.

The main part of the bike is the frame. It is very important in BMXing. The frame is connected to all the other parts of the bike. So it needs to be sturdy. Frames are often made of steel tubes connected by **reinforced** joints.

Handlebars steer the bike. BMX handlebars rise up toward the rider. A brace bar between the handlebars makes them stronger. Handlebars come in different widths. This allows riders of all sizes to find handlebars that will work for them.

The stem is the piece of the bicycle that holds the handlebars. It has two to four bolts that keep the handlebars from slipping or twisting. The bottom of the stem holds the fork. The fork keeps the front wheel in place. The stem and fork must be strong. That is because they absorb most of the

Tire tread

Bike parts

impact when BMXers land jumps. Small arms called pegs flip down from the fork. Pegs are used for freestyle tricks.

Wheels on a BMX bike are made of very strong steel. The wheels are 20 inches (51 cm) in **diameter**. BMX wheels have either 28 to 36 metal spokes, or five wide plastic spokes. BMX tires are made of **knobby** rubber to give the wheel a good grip on the track.

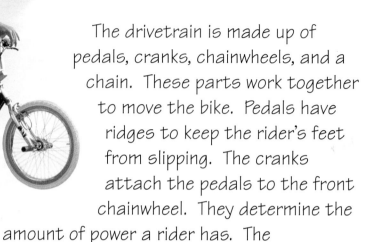

The drivetrain is made up of pedals, cranks, chainwheels, and a chain. These parts work together to move the bike. Pedals have ridges to keep the rider's feet from slipping. The cranks attach the pedals to the front chainwheel. They determine the amount of power a rider has. The chainwheels hold the chain and should **rotate** smoothly. The chain ties the drivetrain together. BMX drivetrains are light but strong.

The hard, narrow seat of a BMX bike is also called the saddle. An adjustable clamp fastens the seat to the seat post. This allows a rider to adjust the seat's height. However, most BMX riders rarely use the seat. Instead, they stand so they can gain more speed while racing and more power while doing tricks.

Brakes are also important on BMX bikes. BMX bikes use caliper brakes. To brake, the rider squeezes a device located near the hand grip. This forces two pads to pinch the edge of the wheel, which slows the bike. All BMX bikes have rear brakes, and some bikes have front brakes, too.

BMX bikes look a lot like regular bicycles, but there are some major differences. One main difference is that a BMX bike usually has only one speed. This means it does not have gears that can shift like many other bikes.

Bikers can pick the types of parts they want on their bikes. Different pieces can be altered to make a bike perfect for its rider. Or, BMX bikes can be purchased already assembled. This is cheaper and less confusing than **custom building** a bike. But an inexpensive bike may not be able to handle the tricks and jumps of BMX biking.

This BMXer is using pegs to perform a trick.

Safety Gear

The thrills of BMX biking can be dangerous. Proper gear is important for safety. Helmets, clothing, gloves, goggles, and bicycle pads will help prevent injuries.

You should have a sturdy helmet that covers your entire head. You should also wear a mouth guard to protect your teeth. Some helmets already have mouth guards attached to them. Others have features that allow you to attach a mouth guard.

You should wear long, thick pants and a long-sleeved shirt when BMXing. They help prevent road rash when you fall. Wear gloves to protect your hands. And wear goggles to keep the dust out of your eyes.

Padding is also needed for your bike. BMX bikes should have pads on the handlebars, crossbar, and stem. This extra padding will help protect you from injury in a fall.

BMX Styles

BMX biking has advanced a lot since children first started popping wheelies. Today, there are different styles of biking that BMXers can do. The main styles are racing and freestyle.

In BMX racing, riders speed around a track. They compete for the fastest time, while still doing some tricks. The tracks are short and made of dirt. They include jumps, curves, downhill sections, whoop-de-doos, and berms. These make the tracks challenging and show each rider's talents.

BMX racers are split into age groups. The groups begin with six-year-old **divisions**. Each age group is then split into **categories**. The categories are beginner, novice, and expert.

At a typical competition, riders compete in three laps called motos. The rider who wins two out of three motos wins the race for his or her category. A biker who wants to advance to the next level must compete in several races. After winning eight races in one year, he or she can advance to the next category.

Downhill BMX racing is also gaining popularity. Riders race down a series of hills and jumps. They compete to see who can ride the fastest. This can be dangerous, so only fully padded, advanced riders should attempt this type of racing.

An early BMX race

Several types of freestyle BMXing are popular. They are called vert, flatland, street, and mini BMXing.

The term *vert* is short for the word *vertical*. In vert BMXing, bikers use a quarter-pipe or half-pipe to catch air. BMXers ride up and down the ramp, gaining speed to do aerials. Vert BMXing is challenging. So beginners should learn the basics before they attempt vert riding. And BMXers should always wear safety gear.

Flatland BMXing is performing in an open area. Empty parking lots are popular places for flatland riding. Bikers do **stunts** with their bikes as their only tool. Wheelies and bunny hops are great flatland tricks for beginners to learn.

Bikers can also use street objects to do tricks. This is called street riding. Curbs, small hills, and railings are used to do tricks. Mini BMXing is when street riders perform on small courses. These courses may have half-pipes, funboxes, and rails. They are very similar to skateparks.

Tricks

bunny hop

This trick is a jump from flat ground. It is done without a launching ramp.

endo

An endo is a front-wheel wheelie or a forward somersault off the bike.

360

A 360 is a complete spin in the air.

superman

A rider does a superman when he or she leaps off a ramp and stretches horizontally in the air while holding onto the handlebars.

bar hop

In this trick, the rider's legs go over the handlebars and through his or her arms.

table top

This is a trick where the rider turns the bike into a horizontal position in the air.

wheelie

A wheelie is riding or balancing with the front wheel off the ground.

truck driver

In a truck driver, the rider does a 360 while also spinning the handlebars 360 degrees.

Lingo

berm

A berm is a banked turn.

aerial

An aerial is any stunt done in midair.

crash and burn

To crash and burn is to fall off a bike.

whoop-de-doos

Whoop-de-doos are a series of small, closely spaced track jumps.

20-incher

This is another name for a BMX bike. It refers to the diameter of the wheels.

holeshot

The holeshot is the lead position at the beginning of a race.

moto

A moto is a qualifying lap.

freestyle

Freestyle is a BMX style where riders perform stunts and tricks in competitions.

skatepark

A skatepark is an area specifically set up for BMXers to practice in. It can be either indoors or outdoors.

cruiser

A large BMX bike is called a cruiser.

half-pipe

A half-pipe is two quarter-pipes placed together to form half of a circle.

quarter-pipe

A quarter-pipe is a curved ramp.

vert

Vert is a style of BMX in which bikers use ramps to perform tricks.

funbox

A funbox has four ramps, one on each side of a box. It is used in street courses.

23

Famous BMXers

The sport of BMX biking has gained popularity thanks to the efforts of several **dedicated** athletes. A few BMXers stand out as leaders. They have worked to make their sport what it is today.

Scot Breithaupt is considered the **founding father** of BMX biking. He began promoting BMX while he was still a teenager. In 1970, at the age of 13, Breithaupt held the first neighborhood BMX races in Long Beach, California.

In the mid-1970s, Bob Haro began the first freestyle team. He is also a talented artist. He used his talents to create colorful, personalized number plates for bikers.

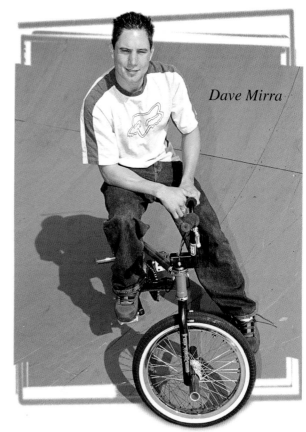

Dave Mirra

After BMX biking became an official sport, Dave Clinton became one of its biggest stars. He took part in many competitions. He even created some of the moves that are still popular today.

Mat Hoffman has participated in BMX biking since 1982. His vert skills are often considered the best in the world. He has won many contests and has created more than 100 tricks. He has even performed in the Olympic ceremonies.

Cindy Davis was one of the best female competitors in racing. Her efforts have encouraged other girls and women to join BMX competitions. By the time Davis retired in 1998, she had received 350 national wins.

BMXer Dave Mirra, also known as "Miracle Boy," has become one of the sport's most recognized athletes. Mirra started riding his bike at age four and has been biking ever since. He quickly mastered the vert slopes. He had a **sponsor** at the age of 13.

Over the years, Mirra has invented and improved many BMX biking **stunts**. He was the first rider to land a double back flip in competition. He has more X Games gold medals than any other athlete. In 2001, Mirra was voted BMX Rider of the Year at the ESPN Action Sports & Music Awards.

BMX Today

Today, BMX competitions are held worldwide. One of the most famous competitions for freestyle BMXing is the X Games. The X Games have exposed extreme sports to many people. This has increased the popularity of BMX biking.

The X Games started in 1995. In these games, several competitions focus on different BMX styles. Some of these styles include downhill, flatland, and park competitions. Hundreds of other competitions occur worldwide throughout the year.

Other famous competitions include the American Bicycle Association races and the NBL races. BMX is an exciting and ever-changing sport. As BMX biking advances, new and more challenging styles of competition will develop. As long as people continue to ride their bikes, BMX biking will remain a popular sport!

Glossary

category - a group in a system of classification.

craze - something that is popular for a short time.

custom build - to make something to fit the individual wants or needs of a single person.

dedicated - committed to a goal or way of life.

diameter - the distance directly through the center of a circle.

division - a competitive class of a sport.

founding father - an originator of an institution or movement.

impact - the force of one object landing on or hitting another.

knobby - covered with rounded lumps or parts that stick out.

market - to sell or advertise a product.

reinforce - to strengthen with additional assistance, material, or support.

rotate - to turn around a central point.

sponsor - a company that provides a BMXer with money for wearing its clothing and using its equipment during a competition.

stunt - an act that is done to attract attention, especially one showing strength, skill, or courage.

trophy - an object awarded for some achievement, such as a sporting event.

version - a different or changed form of something.

Web Sites

Would you like to learn more about BMX biking? Please visit **www.abdopub.com** to find up-to-date Web site links about this sport and its competitions. These links are routinely monitored and updated to provide the most current information available.

Index